RORY AND THE SNACK DRAGONS

Louisa MacDougall

Illustrated by Giulia Cregut

LITTLE DOOR BOOKS

For Mum and Dad

Louisa MacDougall

To my fangtastic husband Matteo!

Giulia Cregut

Thanks to Louisa for writing such a fantastic story and to Giulia for bringing it to life.

Extra special thanks to our amazing designer Gussie for her talents and creativity. You will always be a part of Little Door Books.

Little Door Books

First published in 2024 in Great Britain
by Little Door Books

www.littledoorbooks.co.uk

Text © 2024 Louisa MacDougall

Illustrations © 2024 Giulia Cregut

A CIP catalogue record for this book is available from the British Library upon request

ISBN: 978-1-7391929-3-8

Design and layout by Augusta Kirkwood

Printed in Lithuania by Balto

CONTENTS

CHAPTER 1

"Bleuk!"

Rory the dragon spat out a shiny, pink shoe and hid it under a rock. He glanced both ways to check that none of the other dragons were watching him. It was evening, and his clan were having breakfast. Except it wasn't exactly breakfast, because there was no food.

Normally, the dragons in Rory's clan

ate princesses, for breakfast, lunch, and dinner (with the odd little duchess as a snack between meals) but for weeks now, they hadn't caught one. Today, as there was none of their favourite food available, they were chewing tutus and biting off bits of old ballgown, which, judging from the amount of spluttering going on, was not very tasty.

Rory didn't care whether breakfast was real princess or just princess accessories – he only pretended to eat it anyway. His tastes were different from the other dragons, and he couldn't understand why they enjoyed devouring dainty humans so much.

All those strings of lumpy jewellery

"Eurgh!"

And the silky petticoats "Pah!"

Rory had never mentioned to the other dragons that he hated their disgusting diet (he had nibbled a toenail once, and that had been quite enough). He just hid the evidence and carried on chomping and chewing. Luckily, as it was usually dark, and he was so little (just about rhinoceros-sized) nobody noticed that his jaws were empty.

* * *

"WHERE IS MY BRINGER OF BONES!" thundered a voice. Rory whimpered and slunk deeper into the shadows.

"RORY! GET OUT HERE AND FETCH ME SOME DRUMSTICKS!"

Even the rocks shook when Big Beastly roared.

Big Beastly was the chief dragon. He was as big as a basking shark, as loud as a lion and lazier than either. He was also Rory's uncle.

Being a member of the chief's family made Rory a sort-of dragon prince. But being the youngest, smallest member of this chief's huge family made him feel like anything but royalty.

As soon as he was old enough to fly, Rory had been given the role of 'Bringer of Bones' – a title which actually made him a sort of dragon dishwasher.

After each meal, his job was to collect the bones, tiaras, glass slippers and other rubbish that the dragons flung to the ground, to clean them (usually with his long tongue) and deliver them back to his uncle. Beastly would select the best bits for his treasure trove, and use the rest for 'crafts' like making spears, toothpicks and booby traps. The chief dragon was very keen on recycling.

"RORY! DRUMSTICKS!" A cloud of flies buzzed around Big Beastly's khaki-green head. They were always there, buzzing and jangling Rory's nerves.

The drumsticks Big Beastly wanted were long, straight bones, with knobbly bits on each end.

But there had been no meat today, so Rory knew he wouldn't find fresh bones. He slunk around the other dragons' feet, ducking to avoid the drool from their spitting contests, and wondering where he might find a quiet corner to escape the chaos.

In the corner of the cavern was a pile of rocks – they would have to do. He picked up two skull-sized stones and dragged them to his uncle's gnarly feet. "No bones, Uncle Sssir," he said, looking at the ground. "But, er, these rocks will echo outstandingly."

Big Beastly glared at his nephew: "Useless!" he said, and he flicked his tail, so that its spike just clipped the tip of Rory's ear.

"Ouch!"

The other dragons sniggered. Rory's scales flushed from red to pink.

The dragon chief turned and banged the stones against a slab of rock, filling the cavern with a drumroll that echoed across the mountains. "TIME TO HUNT!" he roared. His followers banged on their slabs, and chanted: "MEAT, MEAT, MEAT!"

Then they lined up at the mouth of their cave, growled at the claw-shaped moon, and one by one, soared into the night to search for dinner.

Rory waited in his place at the back of the line (he was always last) and counted as he watched them go, his ear still stinging.

Nineteen…

Twenty…

Twenty-one.

When number twenty-one, the second-to-last dragon, had disappeared into the night, Rory turned back into the cavern, found a cosy corner, and curled up for a snooze. Night-time was not his thing. Hunting was so not his thing.

But before you start thinking of Rory as a gentle, vegetariany sort-of dragon, think again. It is true that he chose not to eat royal children, or children of any type, but he had other faults.

He was both a coward (a dangerous thing for a dragon) and a thief (a dangerous thing, full stop).

CHAPTER 2

Rory was up before sunrise to make sure the other dragons didn't catch him out snoozing. He hid behind the rocks at the cave mouth and counted them back into the lair.

Nineteen…

Twenty…

And, last and snappiest…

Twenty-one.

Big Beastly was spitting sparks, the other dragons' wing beats were slow, and they carried nothing but a few strings of stolen sausages. "Don't want sausages, want wee sausagey toes," grumbled Rory's cousin, Chomp.

"Enough whining!" roared Beastly. "Princesses are always hard to catch after winter. Soon the world will be riddled with the little brats again."

Rory frowned – he wondered if the others had noticed that their chief didn't sound as sure of himself as usual. There hadn't been a successful hunt for months, and a tingling in his talon-tips told Rory that the problem was serious.

When the last dragon had landed, Rory

counted another twenty-one seconds – the time it normally took for them all to fall asleep – and watched an abandoned ribcage rattle with the force of a squadron of snores.

That sound meant that the coast was clear. Rory took a long, deep breath. The fresh mountain air smelt like freedom. The horizon was calling. It was time to fly away and find his own, different kind of dinner.

He perched at the cave mouth, ready to soar, when...

"RORY!" A roar stopped him, stone-still.

Rory felt hot, toxic breath on his neck and swivelled slowly around to find himself staring straight into his Uncle's lethal-as-lava, decidedly unsleepy eyes.

***

"How did you find the hunt tonight, Rory?" hissed Big Beastly. "Paris is magnificent by moonlight, is it not?"

Beastly was not known for polite chat, or for ever staying up past sunrise. What was he doing out on the precipice now?

Rory shuffled from one foot to the other and braced himself for a blow – perhaps he was in trouble because the dragons' sleeping slabs weren't grimy enough.

"Err. It was delightful, Uncle Sssir," he said. "Loved the moonlit rooftops. Nice tower."

"HA!" Big Beastly spat. "We went to Athens, you ghastly little gecko. And the fog was thicker than snotty dragon-smoke – we couldn't even see the Acropolis!"

Rory's stomach dropped like bat pellets from the cave roof. He was caught.

He had allowed himself to take a risk, to feel the thrill of freedom, but now he would pay. Whatever punishment was coming his way would be far worse than a tail-spiking.

Rory's eyes darted around the cave – was there any hope of making a quick escape? But a glint of metallic green in the gloom told him that the other dragons were there, lurking behind their leader. There would be no getaway today.

"Tonight, our hunt failed," Beastly spat. The droplets of dribble sizzled as they hit the cave floor.

"The Greek royal family's toddler twincesses escaped unscathed, because there was a GAP in our formation. One of our team LET US DOWN. He wasn't where he should have been. In fact, he wasn't there AT ALL!"

Rory stared at the dusty ground. His red scales flickered to a pale shade of mustard. He wasn't brave enough to look into his Uncle's eyes, but he could still feel himself sweating in the heat of their glare.

Big Beastly picked up two boulders (it seemed he was perfectly capable of finding them when he wanted to) and bashed them together three times.

"I call a gathering of the Dragon Ring," he boomed. "NOW!"

* * *

Rory cowered in the centre of the circle of dragons. After years spent fetching and clearing for them, he still knew that there wasn't one dragon whom he could count on to defend him.

"Rory the Dragon, Bringer of Bones, and my disappointing excuse for a nephew," said Beastly.

"You have always been a lazy, lying little lizard, but tonight, you FAILED more spectacularly than ever. You FAILED to strike when you were needed, you FAILED to do your duty, and you LET THIS CLAN DOWN.

"You have wasted every chance to show backbone and battle-readiness. You dishonour the name 'dragon' – and there is only one punishment to fit that crime…

He stopped, to check that all the dragons were listening.

"Your wings will be clipped."

Rory stumbled backwards.

Beastly paused again, enjoying the gasp of his followers. Then he picked up a piece of charcoal, and scrawled on the cave wall.

Name: Rory Gorey MacDragon (Bringer of Bones)

Crimes: Laziness, Lying, Betrayal

~~Conseqwence Consiqu~~ Punishment: Wings Clipped

Rory's jaw opened and closed, then opened again. Even he hadn't imagined a punishment this terrible. For a dragon to have its wings clipped was the ultimate humiliation – he knew that it was centuries since the punishment had last been given, but hatchlings were still told stories of ancient clippings to frighten them into behaving badly.

This sentence meant that a small, heavy clip, made from brontosaurus bone, would be fixed to the tip of each of his wings. The weight would stop Rory from taking off. Or flying at all. Ever.

And all he had done was skip one hunt (well, all the hunts) and tell one little white lie (ahem, he'd told a whole swarm of them).

"All those in favour, STOMP!" said Beastly.

There was silence, and for half a nanosecond, Rory thought that he might get forgiven, that perhaps the other dragons had appreciated him after all.

But then the cave shook with rumble like double thunder, as an army of his nearest and dearest relations stamped their feet – and condemned him to misery – again, and again, and again.

He was doomed.

Although perhaps not quite yet...

CHAPTER 3

The chief cursed: "Crumbling Craniums! I forgot Great Grand-dragon. CHOMP! THUMP! Go and wake the old boulder-butt – for the sentence to be passed everyone must have a chance to cast a vote."

Chomp and his sister Thump raced to the side of the cavern, where they began poking and prodding at what looked like a huge pile of grey-brown, bumpy rocks.

It was only when the rocks began to rumble, and Thump squealed as a blast of stinging black smoke shot into her bulgy eyes, that it became apparent that the pile was in fact a very elderly, sleeping dragon. An elderly, sleeping dragon who had no interest in getting up to cast a vote.

One golden eye blazed like a headlamp. "Ged away!" he growled, then the eye shut.

Big Beastly spat in the dust again. "That's that," he said. "Great Grand-dragon abstains. SENTENCE PASSED."

"Rory. You have one full day and night to set your affairs in order, then, at sunrise tomorrow, your wings will be clipped. If you do not show up, we will HUNT YOU DOWN!"

Beastly lowered his voice and muttered. "Watching you suffer might be just the entertainment these dragons need to take their minds off their empty stomachs."

He yawned, gave Rory one final thwack with his tail, and prowled off to a sleeping slab, his followers scuttling after him. This time, the snores that echoed off the walls were all real.

Rory stared out at the dawn sky. A sky which would soon be out of his reach for ever.

How could he spend the rest of his life stuck in the lair? How could his own flesh and cold blood do this to him? He'd never harmed anyone (but then he supposed that was the problem).

There was a rumble, like a rockfall, and Rory took in a rare sight – the Great Grand-dragon stood, wide awake, beside him.

"You do have a chance," said the old dragon. "In our tradition, even the worst offenders can be forgiven, if they carry out an act of great service to dragon-kind."

Rory had no idea what an 'act of great service' meant.

"What should I do?" he whispered.

"Your dopey relations may not understand yet, but this clan is facing a famine." Great Grand-dragon rubbed at the rusty-looking scales on his tummy. "The only service that might make a difference now, would be finding food. If

I was in your talons, I would go and catch us a princess."

With that, the old dragon slumped to the ground and closed his eyes. An enormous snore burst from his snout, knocking Rory off his feet and over the ledge into the nothingness below.

Luckily for Rory, the tumble was no big deal – this time. Because there was one (only one) dragonish thing that he was really, really good at.

Flying.

He straightened his wings, righted himself with a helter-skelter twist, and soared into the sunrise.

***

Rory glided south, his ears ringing with the old dragon's words. "If I was in your talons, I would go and catch us a princess."

The Great Grand-dragon had meant well, but the more Rory thought, the more certain he was that he didn't have a chink of a chance of performing an 'act of service' to anyone. He should probably just forget about it and enjoy his final food and final flight – at least for now.

Flying always made Rory feel better. He sucked in a deep breath, and puffed out a slow, settling, blue flame. With just clouds for company, he started to feel calmer. Calm enough to make a plan for the hours ahead. It went something like this:

Step 1: Find food (last meal must be fab-u-lous).

Step 2: Eat and enjoy food (see above).

Step 3: Quickly perform act of service to dragon-kind (would picking a big bunch of flowers to say sorry be enough?)

In order to complete step 1, Rory headed towards his favourite place – Scotland. A land of castles, monsters and mountains. A land of mist (mostly just rain, actually) and mystery, where a bottle-green dragon with purple speckles on his snout can blend in with the forests and glens, and stands a better-than-average chance of catching a decent lunch.

Of course, Rory was currently as red as a double-decker bus, which didn't blend in at all.

He gave his tail a little shake, and just like that, his body switched to green. Only the purple freckles on his nose stayed the same colour.

On this particular, misty morning,

Rory circled, until he spotted a small school by a quiet loch. The perfect target.

He may have chosen differently if he had read the sign:

GLEN SPELLING PRIMARY SCHOOL:
EXCELLENT EDUCATION IN LITERACY, MATHEMATICS AND MAGIC.

Rory positioned himself on the branch of an enormous oak tree beside the gate (he may have been the size of a rhino, but he was lighter and much better at climbing).

He watched and waited as children rode their bikes through the gate. He waited and watched as they parked them, side by side, in the bike rack. And then he saw his prey.

An absolute beauty. Sparkling gold and red, its bell glinting in the sunlight, ruby helmet swinging from the handlebars (and a small, sad-looking child parking it – but that didn't matter to him).

A glob of slimy drool dripped from Rory's tongue and landed on the path.

SPLAT! A teacher walked through it, and slipped on to his bottom.

Rory froze as a group of children pointed and laughed, but... just as he was sure they would look up and see him, the school bell rang.

"BRRRRRING!" and the children jostled their way into school.

If Rory had been paying more attention, he might have noticed the small, sad-looking child being elbowed out of the way by the bigger kids. And he might have noticed that the child didn't, in fact, go into class, but snuck behind the school building to a patch of mud (the school allotment) where she crouched down and started to pull up weeds.

But he wasn't paying attention. All he could think about was that delicious-looking bike.

When the children were safely inside, Rory slunk down from the tree and up to the bike rack. His trophy was locked – but that was no problem to a dragon. A quick snort of flame melted the metal.

He pulled the bike out carefully. The scent of steel had Rory's taste buds tingling. He licked his lips...

But then he heard footsteps behind him, and a shout.

"OI! THAT'S MY BIKE!"

CHAPTER 4

Smokes! thought Rory. I've been seen!

As fast as a firework, he wrapped his tail around the handlebars and shot upwards. In two wingbeats, he and the bike were hovering above the school.

He scanned the playground, searching for whoever had shouted at him – but there was no-one there. Perhaps, after all the stress of the morning, he had imagined it. Rory shrugged, and headed homewards, clutching his meal.

The sun warmed his scales, and the sea was sparkling. Rory soon stopped worrying about whatever had shouted at him and started worrying about tomorrow.

His wings quivered at the thought of the clipping. For any dragon, losing the power of flight would be devastating, but for Rory, it was dreadful – the chance to sneak away from the chaos of the lair and escape to the wide world beyond was what kept him going through hours of boring work and bullying.

Maybe it was the worry, but this journey seemed more effort than usual

– or maybe he had stolen a particularly good quality bike, because it definitely felt heavier than the ones he had taken before. A small boulder-weight heavier.

Rory felt a wheel wobble.

He heard what sounded suspiciously like a shout of joy:

"Waaaa Hoooo!"

He glanced below, and what he saw made him snort so suddenly that he burnt his own nostril-hairs off.

***

Dangling from the beautiful bicycle's back mudguard was a girl.

A human girl, with wild, wavy hair,

speckles on her snout (a bit like his, but not purple) and muddy hands, wearing scruffy school uniform and a backpack, with a garden trowel poking out of the back.

And she wasn't there by accident. In fact, judging from that "Waaaa Hoooo," she might have actually been enjoying herself. Now he thought about it, she looked a bit like that small, sad child from earlier – but this version was all fizzles and spark.

I'm tired. I must be imagining things, thought Rory, and he closed his eyes, counted to twenty-one, and looked again.

She was still there. Grinning.

* * *

Rory landed at his favourite picnic spot, a flat-topped rock beside a crater lake, near the dragons' cave.

It was far enough away that he couldn't be seen from the cavern, but close enough that he could still hear Big Beastly's snores reverberating like a drill across the canyon. He was also very partial to drinking its pure, clear water.

Rory set the bike on a pile of rocks, with the child still attached (he was quite careful, because he didn't want his snack to be damaged).

The girl scrambled to her feet. "That was A-Ma-Zing," she gasped.

Then, no longer smiling, she put her hands on her hips and fixed Rory with an icy glare.

"I'm Flora," said the girl. "That's MY bike. Look!" F-L-O-R-A was scratched in tiny letters under the frame.

"How dare you steal it," she spat. "I worked hard to get that bike. I did chores and saved my pocket money. And I planted seeds and watered and weeded and sold veg at the end of our drive. And I've only had it for a week. And I've only just been allowed to ride it to school. And going downhill with the wind in my hair is my favourite thing ever (apart from flying – flying is my new favourite thing). And...JUST GIVE IT BACK!"

Rory stared. This fierce, shouty little human was putting him off his food. "But I want my lunch," he said. "This lunch."

Maybe she would settle down if he explained. "There's nothing quite like eating a bike... the chewiness of tyres... that smoky flavour of brake cables." Rory picked up the bike with one claw and lifted it to his jaws.

"STOP!" yelled Flora. She was very little, but she was very, very loud.

"Did no-one teach you that stealing is wrong?" she asked.

"Of course not. I'm a dragon." Rory tore off the bike's shiny horn with one skilful snap, tossed it into the air and caught it in his fangs. One gulp and it was gone. HONK!

Flora stamped her foot. "That's enough!" she shouted, then, more quietly. "Please stop."

Rory sighed. It was bad enough that the girl's ramblings had unsettled his starter, but now he was feeling sorry for her – and that could add a bitter taste to the whole of the rest of his meal.

Flora seemed to sense Rory's determination wobble. She tried a different way to get what she wanted.

"You obviously like stealing, so maybe you like gambling too," she said. "How about a bet? I BET that I can serve something that you will like eating more than bikes."

"I bet you can't," he replied. She held up her hand.

"If you promise to not-so-much-as lick my bike for five whole minutes, I will make you a fabulous feast. And if I can find one food in that feast that you like even a bit more than you like the taste of bikes, then I win and you have to give mine back – and promise never to eat another.

Rory was listening. "And if not?" he asked.

"If not, you win, and ..." she sniffed, "and I will let you eat my beloved bike in peace."

Rory was absolutely sure that this child had no hope of making a dent in his love of bicycles, but he was curious to see what she would do next. And although he was really, really hungry, he knew he would enjoy his lunch a lot more if he could eat in peace.

He nodded.

"Let's shake on it," she said, holding out her hand.

Rory tutted.

"Dragons don't shake! A dragon promise must be sealed in spit," he said, and spat green slime on to one claw, holding it out for Flora to shake. She paused for a moment, then spat on her elbow, hooked it around the slimy claw, and shook. The deal was done.

"I'll set a timer," she said.

"No," said Rory. "I'll set the timer."

Flora turned a cog on the side of the bicycle's bell and pointed an arrow to the number five. "Clawsome!" said Rory, impressed.

He scratched a line in the dirt at the shadow of a tall rock, and then drew five more minute marks where the moving shadow would fall. "Clever!" said Flora.

Rory fixed Flora with an amber glare.

Flora fixed Rory with an icy one.

"Ready, steady...GO!" they said.

CHAPTER 5

Flora pulled a picnic blanket and a shimmering silver lunch tin out of her bulging school bag. She slammed the tin noisily on the ground, shook the blanket over it, and muttered:

"Spiggedy Spag and some onions and cheese,
Give us a lunch that's spectacular – please!"

POOF!

The lid of the tin burst with an explosion of smashed cheese and onion crisps. As they floated to the ground, like beige confetti, a flood of overcooked slushy spaghetti strands flowed over the sides of the tin and wiggled away.

Slimeballs! She actually is magical, thought Rory. It's just my luck to have accidentally kidnapped a magical kid instead of a normal one. At least she's not very good at it.

"Slugballs! It is so hard to concentrate when I'm feeling kronky," Flora muttered to herself. The bicycle-bell timer clicked. The shadow moved to the first dirt line.

Flora screwed her eyes shut and tried again.

"Ziggedy Zag and a
fire-breathing beast,
When I lift this lid off,
please give us – a feast!"

This time, the results were remarkable.

First, Flora pulled out plates of sandwiches. Cheese and pickle, tuna and sweetcorn, chocolate spread and jellied eels, then peanut butter, fried eggs and more, served on a choice of sliced bread, tiny pittas or giant baguettes, with veggie sticks and dunkable dips – hummus, salsa and chutneys in all the colours of the rainbow.

Rory sniffed. Something smelled ... OK.

Flora wafted the sandwiches under his snout. "Try one."

The bicycle-bell timer clicked again. The shadow moved to the second dirt line.

Rory picked out a peanut butter baguette, took a tiny bite – and spat it out. He rushed to the loch and guzzled a wheelbarrow-load of water, then spat that out too – all over Flora.

"Sand on cardboard!" he said. "You'll have to do better than that."

She shook herself like a wet puppy,

narrowed her eyes and continued. "Next up, creamy eclairs, perfect pastries, a million-layered pavlova, fancy flapjacks, humongous doughnuts and the richest chocolate cake in history," said Flora, pulling out a dragon-sized platter of each.

"Or fruit?"

She dragged out a basket bigger than she was, loaded with bananas, oranges, grapes, watermelon, pineapple, loquats, mulberries and more. Rory's eyes widened.

"I suppose it wouldn't hurt to try," he said, and popped a bunch of thirty unpeeled bananas in his mouth. There was a pause as he chewed, then wrinkled his snout and shook his head.

Next, he wolfed down five bunches

of grapes, a chocolate cake, six mangos (stones included) and a big box of chocolate eclairs (box included).

Gulp. Frown. Gulp.

"Well?" asked Flora.

"Not bad," he said. "Not better than bikes though."

The bicycle-bell timer clicked. The shadow moved to the third dirt line.

"What is so special about bikes, then?" asked Flora.

"EVERYTHING," said Rory, "but particularly the crunch. That moment, when you bite into the frame and it makes that delicious, snappy, kerrrunch noise, and the flavours burst into your mouth. Crunching is – almost as good a feeling as flying."

"Flying does make you feel incredible," agreed Flora.

The bicycle-bell timer clicked again. The shadow moved to the fourth dirt line. Rory ambled to the lake edge and took another slow, glug of cool water.

She's almost out of time, he thought, if I waste a few more seconds then I've won this bet.

Flora picked up a big, shiny, bright green apple, tossed it in the air, and caught it. It didn't look much to Rory. Winning was going to be so easy.

"If you enjoy crunch, there's nothing quite like a Granny Smith," Flora said.

Rory snapped at her. "Humans are

odd! You think that we are cruel, but even the dastardliest dragon would never eat his own kind – especially not a Granny!"

Flora shook her head and rolled the apple to Rory's feet. "This apple is called a Granny Smith!" she explained. "It is crunchy – but definitely NOT human."

Rory sniffed the fragrant fruit, just to be sure, then speared it with one claw and popped it in his mouth.

KERRRUNCH!

What. A. Fangtastic. Snap.

"Got any more?" he asked. Flora bowled another, and another – until Rory had snapped up three dozen. Each with the same delectable crunch.

"These are terrrrific!" he mumbled, his

mouth bulging and flakes of apple peel stuck on his fangs (dragons have really bad table manners). His scales flickered all the colours of the rainbow.

"Better than a bike?" asked Flora. Juice spraying, he nodded "Schlloop! Way better. Less scratchy."

Brrrrrring! The five-minute bicycle bell rang. The shadow fell on Rory's fifth line.

Flora had won.

CHAPTER 6

"I'll be off then," Flora grinned. "Could you give me my bike back, please – and maybe a sky ride home to Scotland?" She held her arms out wide, like a plane.

"I'm not sure I liked those apples all that much," Rory lied. "I might have room for a pedal pudding..."

Flora scowled. "We had a deal," she said. "We spat on it."

"Slimeballs!" Rory sighed. She was right. A promise made in dragon spit must not be broken.

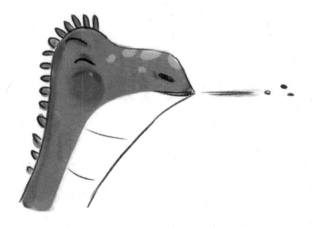

Rory lay back, warming his full tummy in the sun and picking apple pips out of his fangs. Flora lay next to him. It was odd that she didn't seem at all afraid.

He flicked his apple pips over the ledge and into the canyon.

She made a tidy pile with hers.

"You shouldn't waste your pips," she said. "You can grow trees from them, and they will produce more apples."

"Really?" he asked.

Flora nodded and pulled a handful of dried seeds from her pocket, holding them out to show him.

"These are fruit and vegetable seeds – I was going to plant them in the school allotment today," she said. "With light, water and a little bit of goodness, anyone can grow anything. One day, these tiny things will become something amazing – and I will too."

Rory gulped. Amazing was not how he imagined his own flightless future.

"At school," said Flora, "I'm growing an orchard. It's how I keep busy at break-times when the other kids won't play with me. It's full of spindly trees and tiny bushes now – but soon, they'll grow bigger and there will be fruit. If we fly back now, you could come and see."

It didn't cross Rory's mind to ask why the other children wouldn't play with Flora – the other dragons never played with him either. He watched as she tucked the seeds away, spread her arms and zoomed around him in a circle.

"You really can't wait to fly again, can you?" he said.

Flora grinned. "It's even better than cycling," she said, "and I LOVE cycling."

"That whoosh of wind beneath your wings is fangtastic," he agreed. "But just wait until you try a loop-the-loop, the wind rushes round your ears and, for a moment, you feel like you're falling, then you flip and... KER POW! Best. Feeling. Ever!"

"What other tricks can you do?" said Flora, reaching into her rucksack and pulling out a notebook. "I'm going to write them down so I can try myself – one day!"

Rory's eyes sparkled and Flora's grew wider as he talked and she wrote:

Loop-the-Loop: a super-sonic airborne forward roll.

Dive Bomb: plummet to the ground, then pull up at the last moment. Bonus points for scaring someone below.

Triple barrel roll: like a loop-the-loop but sideways x3.

The Quadruple Trump: extra propulsion power. Warning: do not fly behind a dragon who is performing this move. Note: Best with coloured smoke.

"You are clever to do all those tricks," said Flora. "Would you show them to me?"

66

Rory nodded. "That might be fun. No one has ever been interested in watching me fly before."

It was strange, Rory thought. This little girl was loud, irritating and had turned his lunch plans to bone dust, but somehow, the thought of spending a bit more time flying with her wasn't entirely slimesome.

Swift as a sneeze, Flora hopped on her bike and then stared at him, expectant. Rory let out a puff of smoke, launched himself skywards (not quite as quickly as usual, thanks to his full tummy) and then zipped back down, pulling up only a gnat's-width from the top of her head.

"Again!" she laughed.

He repeated the manoeuvre, but this time he grabbed the handlebars and lifted her skywards with him.

"Fangtastic!" she yelled.

They barrel-rolled and dive-bombed and snorted and giggled and finally collapsed in a breathless heap back at the picnic spot.

Nap-time, thought Rory, curling his

body into the usual cosy spiral. But Flora stretched to her tiptoes and peered into the distance.

"Look!" She pointed to a rock, jutting out of the cliff-side high above the loch. "It's shaped just like a diving board! Can you put me up there? I want to try something..."

Huffing, Rory uncurled and lifted Flora and her bicycle to the rock. Perhaps she wants to sketch the view from the top in that notebook of hers, while I rest ready for the journey back, he thought.

He thought wrong.

Tipping the bike into a wheelie, Flora rode along the rock platform, balanced for a fraction of a moment on the edge, and deliberately tumbled straight off into…

Nothing.

In what seemed to Rory like slow motion, she flipped one, two, three perfect backward rolls.

Then plunged down towards the icy water. Rory watched. Jaws open.

"CAAATCH…MEEEEEEeeeee…" she yelled.

Finally realising what was about to happen, Rory shot along the surface of the loch at rocket speed, snapped at the straps of her backpack with his fangs, and – just as her wheel tip dipped into the water – soared upwards and away with Flora and the bike dangling dangerously from his mouth.

"Bwot bwere yoo finking!" he grumbled – a mouth full of backpack – and dropped her, not that gently this time, back on the picnic blanket.

Flora grinned. And though he tried to give her a stern dragon glare, Rory couldn't help grinning back.

The girl may be spine-scratchingly irritating, but he had to admit that she was fun!

Just then, a cloud moved in front of the sun, and Rory saw that the sun wasn't as high as it had been – it was afternoon already.

He may have preferred to swoop through the skies with Flora for the rest of the day, but there were only a few hours left until his wing-clipping punishment.

If he was ever going to fly again, he had to go and perform that act of great service to dragon-kind (like finding Big Beastly a princess to eat) and he had to do it now.

But how would he explain that to Flora?

"Time to take me home!" said Flora, and she opened her backpack to put the picnic blanket away. As she did, something shiny, spiky and studded with jewels fell out and clunked onto a rock.

Rory stared: "What IS that?" he asked, though of course, as soon as he saw it, he knew.

She picked it up. "This?" Flora put the

thing lopsidedly on her head. "That's just my crown."

CHAPTER 7

Rory turned a minty colour.

"They're quite strict about what you wear at school," she chattered. "The rules are: No toys. No phones. No Crown Jewels. So I keep it at the bottom of my bag."

"Spiralling Smokes!" he gasped. "You're a princess!"

"Uh huh," Flora shrugged, not sounding like one.

"But..." spluttered Rory. "You're scruffy... and you ride a bike...and you go to school."

"Uh huh," said Flora again.

"I don't like dresses or hairbrushes. And why shouldn't I have a bike and go to school. At least there are children my own age there (even if they don't actually play with me and call me names like Princess Slug-Sister and Her Royal Sliminess)."

Flora's voice went quiet. "And, there is another reason...

"Princesses from all over the world have been disappearing – in fact, we might be almost extinct." She shrugged. "Mum and Dad thought that if I went to school, dressed like other children, and learned some magic defences, I would blend in and be safer."

Rory's stomach did a loop-the-loop. He knew why those princesses had been disappearing. No princess – not even a scruffy, magical one – was safe here.

Just then, there was a rumble from deep in the cave behind them, and Rory realised that he hadn't heard that drill-like snoring for a while.

A voice roared: "I SMELL BREAKFAST!"

Rory's stomach did a triple barrel-roll. His scales faded, once again, from mint green to mustard yellow.

***

"RORY!" roared Big Beastly's voice. "I smell princess. If you're keeping one to yourself up there, I'll have your scales for sprinkles..."

Rory looked from the princess to the cave mouth and groaned.

The voice sounded closer... almost pleading...

"But if you hand over that delicious little delicacy, right now. You will have carried out an act of great service to dragon-kind – and we can forget all about the little matter of the wing-clipping."

Rory shuddered at the thought of the punishment that was just hours away.

Except now, he slowly realised, it didn't have to be.

Stood beside him, looking confused, was the very thing he needed to win his freedom – and no dragon even needed to know that 'hunting' her had been an accident.

If he handed Flora to Big Beastly now, he could be a hero: the dragon who provided a princess when no-one else could. The dragon who saved dragon-kind from starvation. He would finally be accepted. One of the clan.

But the thought of anyone eating Flora felt like a talon squeezing his heart. He closed his eyes and remembered their picnic, and the chat (no one had ever 'chatted' with him before) and her orchard plans, and most of all, the thrill of flying together.

He took a long, shuddering breath. One, two, three.

Then held it for a moment as he made his mind up, then shakily, smokily, let it go – along with all his hopes of flight or freedom.

"Get on the bike," he hissed, then

without waiting for her to move, he picked Flora up, plonked her on to her bike, then grabbed the helmet and frisbeed that towards her head too. "They want to eat you. You have to get away – NOW."

He pointed the bike down a mountain path. "Pedal for your life!"

Rory gave her a quick shove down the slope and turned to duck behind a (not particularly big) round boulder, near the mouth of the lair.

Just then, a snout emerged from the cave mouth: "I CAN SEE YOU, YOU SNIVELLING SALAMANDER! GET OUT FROM BEHIND THAT PEBBLE!"

"There's n-n-nothing here, Uncle," lied Rory, uncurling his tail and spreading his wings to block the view below. "Your nostrils must be deceiving you. I'm just getting ready to start my quest. You know, the act of great service thingy. I'm sorry if me talking-to-myself disturbed you."

Rory edged backwards, hoping that his mumbling would buy Flora enough time to escape.

And then hoping that he hadn't heard what he thought he had heard – the scrunch of gravel spraying behind him.

Ding Ding!

The bicycle bell rang and a breathless Flora did a wheelie as she reappeared on the cliff-edge. Slimeballs! It seemed she had not understood Rory's plan for her escape.

"Do all princesses like danger for dinner, or is it just you?" he snapped as she screeched to a stop beside him. The girl did nothing quietly.

"You are such a tetchy reptile," she stage-whispered back.

Big Beastly squeezed his barrel-like tummy through the cave mouth and stomped towards them, flies still buzzing above his head. Flora leaned against Rory's neck.

"There's no way I was going to leave you to face that horrid dragon alone," she said. "I'm tired of hiding from bullies – and I can do a bit of magic. We'll stand up to him together."

The other dragons loomed behind

Beastly. Rory shook his head. "Running away beats standing up every time," he said. "Fancy another flight?"

Then Rory did something he would never have considered a few hours earlier. He dipped his head, gritted his teeth and pushed the boulder he had been hiding behind with his snout – straight towards

Big Beastly. Then he grabbed the bike, back-to-front, with Flora still sat on the saddle, and took off.

"Since I met you, I have started doing some very strange things," he said.

CHAPTER 8

"What's happening, Flora," asked Rory. "Why aren't they chasing us."

There was a bellow from below.

"That boulder's trapped one of the big dragon's claws," said Flora. "The others are rolling it off him now... His whole body has changed colour from green to a kind of maroony red... Is that a bad sign?

"That's it, they've rolled it off now. Here they come, Rory. Hurry!"

Rory was already hurrying. He was proud of his skills and speed, but without help, he knew that stronger dragons would catch him up eventually.

"Now would be an excellent time for some of that magic you mentioned," he said. "How about flaming arrows? A thunderbolt or two?"

Flora went unusually quiet. For one, two, three wing beats. Then...

"The thing is," she mumbled, "I've been at magic school for four weeks. Supper Sorcery is the only topic we've studied – it's the only magic I can do!"

"Oh, Smokes!" said Rory. "I suppose

you'd better give that a try – go on, do something. Quick!"

Flying fast, with a back-to-front bicycle in your talons isn't easy at the best of times. Flying fast, with a back-to-front bicycle in your talons, while not dropping a wriggling princess who is trying to pull a tin out of her bag, is almost impossible.

But Rory was really very good at flying. He held his shaky course and Flora shook the magical tin in the direction of the approaching dragons. "There are twenty-one of them, and only two of us," she muttered. "This is so not fair!"

"Get on with it, Flora!" panted Rory.

So she tried.

"Um. Flaky pastry and
big black hole,
Turn wingy thingies
into sausage rolls..."

There was a tiny "zzzip" as five of the flies that always followed Beastly turned into tiny pastries and plummeted to the ground. "Arrrgh!" said Flora, and shook her fist at Big Beastly. "Horrid Beast! It is so hard to concentrate when I'm feeling fraggly!"

Big Beastly snapped at the space where her fist had been a moment before.

"Flora," said Rory. "We really need your magic to work. When my tummy's all jumbly, I take a deep breath, then concentrate really hard on the tip of my nose and let it out as a slow, blue flame. It helps me to feel a bit better. Could you try something like that?

Flora took a slow breath in, closed her eyes then puffed the air out. Then again.

"That would be way better with an actual flame," she grumbled but she did sound a bit calmer.

She hugged the enchanted tin to her chest and muttered the spell that had worked for her earlier.

"Ziggedy Zag and a
fire-breathing beast,
When I lift this lid off,
please show me – a feast!"

This time she pulled out a tray full of cherry pies.

She lobbed them at the dragons one by one.

SPLAT! SPLAT! SPLAT!

"It's not ammunition, it's yummunition!" she giggled.

Surprise slowed the dragons' pace for a second, but the blood-red cherry juice dripping from the dragons' wings made them look even more terrifying.

"Ooh, here are some cucumbers!" Flora threw the long, green missiles next, but sharp wing-tips simply spliced them into circles.

CHOP! CHOP! CHOP!

"Find something harder," Rory yelled.

"How about coconuts?" said Flora. She took aim.

CHAPTER 9

"DOINK!"

A coconut hit Big Beastly. He headed it like a football into a crater.

"DOINK!"

Another hit Chomp's armoured foot. He kicked it to the dragon behind him, Thump, who flipped to catch it with her mouth, and hooked the third coconut with her tail.

"COCO-BALL!" The dragons yelled.

The coconuts may not have caused any damage, but for a few seconds the dragons were distracted as they played a more violent version of dodgeball – passing the hard, husky balls back and forth as they tried to knock each other hard on the head. The longer they played, the more chance Rory had to put some distance between them.

But a dragon's attention span is shorter than the time it takes one to swallow a skull, and soon, they started to try a new game.

"COCO-CANNON!" called Chomp, catching a coconut in his mouth and spitting it, with frightening force, at the escaping duo. The others copied.

PA-PA-PA-PA! The canyon exploded in a barrage of nutty ammunition.

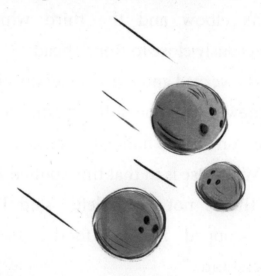

"DUCK!" yelled Flora.

"It's really not the time for bird-spotting, Flora," replied Rory, turning his head. "I need to concentrate on escap.... OH, I see."

He ducked, just in time.

Most of the spat nuts were aimed badly, but Big Beastly's second coconut grazed Flora's elbow and the third whistled dangerously close to Rory's head.

He swerved and twirled and dived, but he knew it could be only a matter of time before one of the nuts hit its target.

"What else is in that tin?" puffed Rory.

"There's not much left!" said Flora. "It's stopped making food... I don't understand..."

The sun was starting to set. Flora stared at it, then slapped her forehead.

"Carrot-tops! I forgot that there are limits on supper sorcery to stop students from snacking before bedtime. The tin stops working after dinner-time at school... Dinner-time must be over!"

Rory groaned. "Is there anything left at all?" Flora reached into the tin and snatched her hand out: "Ugh! Only boiled Brussels sprouts! Squishy and healthy, but no use in a fight!"

Rory inhaled a familiar scent – rubber. The heat of Beastly's breath was starting to melt the bicycle tyres and the rubber soles of Flora's school shoes. He had almost caught up with them.

"What now, Rory?" asked Flora. "We CANNOT let those bullies win." She bashed her hands crossly on to the handlebars. The bicycle bell rang "DING!"

The sound gave Rory an idea. "I think there could be a use for those sprouts," he said, and whispered his plan.

***

Flora placed one squishy, round sprout on the ringer of the bell, pulled it back, and fired!

DING-A-LING!

The bell catapult gave the little sprout both speed and spin. It hit Big Beastly smack in the middle of his forehead, sending green sludge into his eyes.

SQUELCH!

"Yes!" said Flora, making a fist with one hand.

But what happened next surprised them all.

Stunned, the giant dragon's jaws fell open, and the sprout mush slipped down his snout and dropped into his mouth.

There was silence, then, like a whale-sized chameleon, Big Beastly's scales changed, flashing from khaki, to purple, to gold, and finally settling at a sunny sort-of orange. Rory had never seen him that colour before.

"It couldn't be… Surely not… You don't think he actually likes it?" asked Flora.

"I'm not sure," said Rory. "When a dragon's skin changes colour it is definitely a sign of strong feelings – but I don't know which ones!"

As if he had heard them, the chief dragon

licked his lips. "SCRUMPTASTIC!" he yelled.: "GIVE ME MORE!"

Flora fired a round of sprouts from the bell into Big Beastly's mouth. Then she aimed another load from left to right, so the other dragons all got a taste.

BRRRRRRING-A-LING-A-LING-A-LING!

"SQUISHILICIOUS!" snorted Chomp.

"SLUDGETACULAR!" agreed Thump.

Flora and Rory kept feeding the dragons Brussels sprouts until there were none left.

"MORE!" the dragons roared. But this time the tin really was empty.

Flora tipped it upside down, and shook. Nothing. She shook harder, but she lost her grip and it fell, bounced off a rock and vanished into a pool of quicksand.

"THAT JUST TICKLED MY TASTEBUDS. I'M STILL HUNGRY!" said Big Beastly.

A ring of flying dragons surrounded the pair. Their eyes glaring with hunger – and anger. There was nowhere left to go.

"Rory, I don't want to be eaten," said Flora. He draped his tail gently around her shoulders. The last rays from the setting sun bathed the canyon in amber light.

A dragon-sized tear splashed onto the dusty ground.

A little-girl-sized tear splashed beside it.

Then something incredible happened.

CHAPTER 10

Where their salty tears soaked the ground, a green shoot appeared.

In seconds, the shoot grew two leaves, then four, then it became a tree, which grew to the height of a small child, then a small rhinoceros-sized dragon – then a big, bus-sized dragon.

The moment it stopped growing, the tree blossomed with delicate pink flowers, which were replaced by fruit, and before a minute was up, its branches sagged with the weight of dozens of bright green, shiny apples.

Flora and Rory gazed. The other dragons gaped – enchanted into forgetting their hunt for a moment.

"Rory," whispered Flora. "I didn't do any magic!"

He fluttered gently downwards and they landed below the tree. It felt safe in the shade beneath its branches and the other dragons didn't follow. Rory gazed up through the lacy pattern of the leaves.

"Maybe you did do magic – without realising," he said. "or maybe WE did. What was it you said before? 'Anyone can grow anything, with light, water and a bit of goodness.'

"Look. We've got sunlight, and water..."

She nodded. "And is it possible that our friendship could be the little bit of goodness?"

Rory sniffed. Their friendship. He'd never had a friend before. It would be a nice thing to remember when he was trapped, forever flightless, in the dragon's lair.

The scent of apples caught Rory's nostrils, and he smiled as he remembered how Flora had beaten him in their bet, with her deliciously crunchy Granny Smiths.

And that gave Rory another idea.

He had to make sure his friend would be safe, before his wings got clipped and he couldn't swoop in to save her from danger ever again.

"What now, Rory?" she asked. "I'm guessing that you have another plan?"

* * *

Flora climbed off the bike and onto Rory's back, then she shouted, at the top of her tiny, powerful lungs, at the still gobsmacked dragons.

"OI!" she said. "ARE YOU STILL HUNGRY?"

Twenty-one dragon heads nodded. "WELL, TOUGH TURNIPS! THOSE SPROUTS HAVE GONE. AND YOU ARE NOT ALLOWED TO EAT ME!"

Twenty-one growls rumbled. Flora continued, her voice hardly quivering at all. "IF YOU DON'T EAT ME, I CAN HELP YOU TO GROW MORE!"

Big Beastly stomped towards them and Flora stopped talking. Rory gulped – their plan wasn't working... yet, but this time, he was going to stand his ground. With his friend. It might be too late to save his wings – but there was a chance to save her skin.

He stepped forward.

"Uncle," he said. "I AM NOT going to let you eat Flora." He gulped, but kept talking.

"Not just because in one afternoon she has been kinder to me than you have in my whole life, but because I want you, and the rest of my family, to think about what is going to happen after you have eaten her.

"I think it's time the other dragons found out what we both know – that, because of dragons' greed, princesses are almost extinct. It's possible that Flora here is the last one.

There was a group gasp, and this time, you could have heard a tooth drop, as Rory's shaky voice rose. "Soon, you will all start to starve."

"I WILL NOT let you eat my friend, but I WILL ask her to help you. Flora is a fantastic gardener. She knows everything we need to know to grow our own food.

Food like the sumptuous sprouts that you just ate, and these incrrrredible apples. Food that – if we are careful with how we grow it – will not ever run out.

"You will be able to eat and keep on eating – without doing any harm. But... if Flora is going to help you, you must promise not to eat her. Not now, not later, and not EVER."

The other dragons turned on their chief. "Is it true, Beastly?" "Are the princesses all gone?" "How could you not tell us?"

Big Beastly stepped forward and stood snout to snout with Rory. He raised his front leg. Rory winced, ready for the blow.

CHAPTER 11

The chief slapped his nephew on the back. Hard. The mountains rang with the echo of his booming laugh. "Well, well, well!" he chuckled.

"DRAGONS! Do as my nephew asks. Finally, he has shown us that he can stand up for himself."

Big Beastly dribbled a big blob of slimy green saliva onto his machete-like claw, then held it out for Rory to hook. "I promise not to eat your friend," he said.

As you know, a promise sealed with dragon spit can never be broken. Flora was safe.

***

"Flora," said Rory, as they flew back to the dragons' lair. "The dragons are hungry already. Are we going to be able to grow enough food in time? Doesn't it take months?"

"I've been thinking about that," said Flora, "and about what you said at the magic apple tree. I think it grew from one of those pips you flicked at lunchtime.

And I think you could be right that it grew so fast because of the goodness in our tears.

"I'm not feeling so sad now, and neither are you, judging from the rosy colour of your scales, so I think we'll just have to find something else that has lots of goodness in it, to give us the growing power we need."

On the flat ground below the dragons' cave, Flora showed her twenty-one apprentice gardeners how to rake dust with their claws, and Rory taught them to collect seeds from leftovers. Flora shared the seeds that she had been keeping in her pocket – runner beans, Brussels sprouts, strawberries and cauliflowers, and the dragons scattered them by moonlight.

After a while Flora noticed that dragons kept disappearing. They would be gone for a few moments and would then come back. "Where are they going to?" she asked Rory, whose scaly purple-speckled cheeks flushed a darker red. "They just need to be private, to er, have a think," he said.

Flora frowned, confused, and then she understood – and chuckled. "Rory, that's exactly what we need!" she said. "Show me where they go!"

Rory led Flora to the 'private place' behind the cavern, her nose wrinkling as they got closer. "Is this what you need?" he asked. There, steaming like boiled vegetables, was a mountain of dragon poo.

"Goodness!" Flora grinned. She gathered the dragons, and using coconut shells as shovels, they collected the dung and spread it over their seeds.

As the sun rose, it started to rain. "Light, water and... a little bit of goodness," yawned Rory.

"Cross your talons that this works," said Flora, rubbing her eyes, and, right at the mouth of the dragons' cave, they curled up and fell asleep.

***

It was late afternoon when the clatter of dragon chatter woke Rory and Flora. It was almost sunset. How could he have slept so long?

Rory's stomach looped-the-loop and even slowly breathing a blue flame wouldn't settle it. It was almost time.

"BREAKFAST!" roared Big Beastly. Flora dived under Rory's tail.

But she wasn't the breakfast the dragons

were interested in. Their eyes followed the sound of Beastly's roar.

Stretching across what yesterday had been a dusty canyon, were rows and rows of jumbo-sized vegetables: runner beans, Brussels sprouts and cauliflowers, and beside the tree that had stood alone yesterday, a grand orchard packed with apples and pears, with strawberries on the ground below.

The dragons zoomed in formation down the canyon, and started to harvest the healthiest, tastiest meal that had ever passed their lips. Amid the belching and lip-smacking, only Rory was quiet.

"What's up, Rory?" asked Flora. "It worked! Aren't you delighted?"

He smiled. "I am. But there's something I need to tell you, Flora. I'm afraid you might have to cycle all the way home – I'm not going to be able to fly you back."

She dropped the pear she had been chomping. "Oh."

Just then, Big Beastly stomped towards them, a bush of Brussels sprouts tucked behind his ear, his dagger-like teeth flecked with broccoli. He held a brontosaurus bone clip in his claw.

"RORY GOREY MACDRAGON, BRINGER OF BONES!" he boomed.

"I will not be a coward. I will not be a coward," Rory said. He stepped forward to meet his uncle.

"I know it's time," he said. "I know I

failed to provide a princess for dinner. I know I was lazy and cowardly and told lies. I'm ready for my punishment." He gulped and held forward the tips of both his wings.

Big Beastly laughed so hard that fruit thudded from the trees. "Rory! I haven't come to punish you," he said.

There was a rumble of rocks and Great Grand-dragon creaked up to stand beside the chief, one cheek puffed out with what looked like a whole cauliflower.

"A princess on a platter might have been nice, but in ancient dragon law, you needed to carry out any 'act of great service to dragon-kind,'" he reminded Rory.

Big Beastly swept his great wing out

over the desert that, overnight, had become a farm. "I think we can agree that you have done that. THERE WILL BE NO WING-CLIPPING TODAY."

Beastly picked up a sharpened stick and shoved it into the ground next to a flourishing runner bean plant. Then he joined the stick and the plant together, with a click of the bone clip. "That should help it to grow straight," he said.

Rory breathed out a slow, beautiful, curling blue flame. His tummy loops had stopped. Flora stood on tiptoes and kissed his scaly cheek (which, for just a moment, flushed golden).

Big Beastly coughed. "Actually," he said. "I came with a promotion." He raised his voice. "BRINGER OF BONES!" he said. "I HEREBY PROMOTE YOU TO EXCALIBUR OF THE EXCREMENT... No, that's not quite right. PROTECTOR OF THE POTTY PILE. No, I've got it. GUARDIAN OF THE GUANO!"

Rory puffed out his chest – this sounded like a great honour – but Flora nudged him. "He wants you to look after all the poo!" she said.

Rory spluttered. "Err. I'll think about it," he said.

CHAPTER 12

That night, Beastly held a Brussels sprout banquet to thank Flora and Rory (they may have been the guests of honour, but he chose the menu). There was a sprout trifle, Scotch sprouts, sprout cake, sprout spread on sprout toast, and a terrific pyramid of soft boiled Brussels sprouts.

Rory was sat at the place of honour between his uncle and a surprisingly sprightly Great Grand-dragon, and for the first time, the other dragons included him in their long-distance spitting contests (he was nowhere near as good as Flora, but it was fun to try).

Once the dragons' bellies were full, they rolled on to their backs to rest. This time the noise in the cave wasn't just the rumble of snores. It was the rumble of gas escaping from dragon bottoms.

"Are you ready for a sky ride?" Rory asked Flora, whose face was turning a distinctly dragony shade of green.

Flora put on her helmet and hopped on to the bike. Rory grabbed the handlebars.

"Fangtastic!" they yelled.

They triple barrel-rolled upwards and soared into the stars.

***

Flora's mum and dad were startled when their daughter was delivered to the castle roof on a bicycle gripped in a dragon's claws, but they were used to her quirky ways. Once she had persuaded the royal knights to lower their spears and filled her family in on her adventures, they welcomed Rory into their home.

"I shall send a proclamation to tell the other royal families that our princesses are safe at last," said King Colin. "There are girls like you in hiding all over the world, Flora. On rugby camps and at racing tracks – I think there's even one on the International Space Station.

"They will be so relieved to come home, put their flouncy dresses back on and go back to attending posh tea parties," he said.

Flora opened her mouth to argue – the space station sounded like a lot of fun and she had never been that fussed about flouncy dresses or tea parties – but Queen Grace gave her daughter a big, twinkly wink, so she decided not to say anything – yet.

Perhaps she wasn't the only princess who had rather enjoyed her time away – and perhaps hiding from dragons hadn't been the only reason that the queens had asked for their daughters to be sent under cover. The matter of what princesses really enjoyed could stay their secret – for now.

Later, Flora showed Rory the castle orchard. It wasn't as big as the dragons', but it was full of beautiful tiny trees, plum and pear, quince and apricot and, of course, crunchy Granny Smith apples.

"These are even better than the magic ones," he said, spraying her with juice, as bits of apple peel got stuck in his fangs – again.

"I could collect some pips for you to take back," she replied. "Unless..."

He looked at his friend. "Unless?"

"Unless you'd like to stay for a bit. I'm

sure mummy would find you a job – if you don't want to be Big Beastly's toilet keeper, that is."

Queen Grace did indeed have the perfect job for Rory.

***

He set up a workshop in the dungeon and Flora made him a sign.

RORY'S
BICYCLE REPAIRS.

FREE SERVICE AND LESSONS
FOR ALL CHILDREN.

BY ROYAL APPOINTMENT.

Rory was very good at his new job. His claws made super screwdrivers and dragon flames were the perfect temperature for welding broken spokes.

When children came to get their bikes fixed, they chatted to Flora and practised tricks with her and she found that they soon stopped treating her like a princess and started treating her as a friend.

When Rory was hungry, he was free to help himself from the palace gardens, or to join the royal family for a feast in the great hall. Sometimes they would meet him for a barbecue in the grounds (no need for charcoal when your host is a dragon). True to his promise, he didn't so much as nibble at the bikes he was asked to repair.

If the royal family were hosting a grand event at which extra-impressive food was required, they would request a hamper of Beastly's Brussels sprouts from the dragons' super-successful farm, and Rory and Flora would fly back to visit and collect the order. While once Beastly had used Rory as a dishwasher, now he was an honoured friend – greeted with piles of presents made from old bones that the dragons no longer wanted.

And so their happy ending unfolded, until one morning, Flora went to fetch her bike to ride to school – and discovered that it was not in the royal bike rack. Her heart sank like a sky-diving sausage roll. Could Rory have returned to his old, thieving ways?

She searched the palace and the grounds, and then, hearing a clank that confirmed her fears, she crept to the dungeon. She tiptoed to the cell that was Rory's workshop and peered through the bars.

Pieces of what looked like her bike were spread around the floor. A cog here, a spring there. But there was no sign of the dragon, or the bicycle.

Finally, Rory appeared, a black smear of grease on one scaly cheek. "Flora! I wasn't expecting you." He flashed his fangs. "But I'm almost finished – come and see."

She followed him to a nearby cell, where something covered with a well-used picnic blanket hung from the ceiling.

"I wanted to make a gift," he said. "To say thank you for being my friend.

"I know you love cycling, and we both love flying . . . so I've just made a couple of little adjustments to your bike, and now...

"Ta da!"

Rory pulled off the blanket, and there

it was. Her bike. Still an absolute beauty. Still sparkling gold and red, with its bell glinting in the lantern light. But now, attached to the frame were two, huge feathery wings, made from the dried leaves of jumbo Brussels sprouts. Flora would be able to fly.

"Well?" asked Rory.

"I love it!" Flora shouted. She wasn't very big, but she was very, very loud.

Rory grabbed her helmet and frisbeed it towards her head. "Come on," he said. "Let's go for a sky ride!"

THE END

RORY'S
ROARSOME (ROARFUL) DRAGON JOKES

What's the one thing
a dragon can play
on the piano?

SCALES

Why did the
snowman fall
in love with the
dragon?

BECAUSE SHE MELTED
HIS HEART

How do dragons
like to eat their
vegetables?

ROAR

What do you say to a dragon who toasts marshmallows for you?

FANGS A LOT

What's a dragon's favourite entertainment?

A TALONS SHOW

How can you find out what a dragon weighs?

USE THE SCALES!

What's the sound of an angry dragon on an ice rink?

SPLASH!

Why is it a mistake to befriend a dragon?

BECAUSE SHE'S HERE TODAY, DRA-GONE TOMORROW

FLORA'S APPLE PIP GROWING TIPS

You will need:

- An apple
- Compost or soil
- A yoghurt pot or similar-sized container (ask a grown-up to poke holes in the bottom for you)
- A loo roll (minus the toilet paper)
- A paper towel or kitchen roll
- A small plastic (e.g. sandwich) bag or pocket

Step 1:

Eat your apple. Chomp. Chomp. Dribble.

Step 2

Put your pips on the paper towel and let them dry. Wrap the pips up in the towel.

Step 3

Put a few drops of water onto the paper towel/kitchen roll, or dip the package in a cup of water, so that it is damp but not soaking wet.

Put the pips and the paper towel package into the bag.
Put your bag in the fridge and trick the pips into thinking that it is winter.

Step 4

Wait. You can check on your bag sometimes and add a bit more water to keep it damp, but the next bit takes six to ten weeks. Zzzzzzz. Eventually, you should see the seeds crack and a root shoot appear.

Step 5

Fill your yoghurt pot with compost or soil (make sure your grown-up put those holes in the bottom) and pop your shooting apple pips in, about a fingernail length below the surface.
Place it in a warm, light spot, like on a windowsill, and watch it grow. Water every few days.

Step 6

When your tiny tree has two sets of leaves, transplant it. Cut the toilet roll in half and pinch the bottom to make a tiny, biodegradable pot, then gently move the seedling in, with its roots.
Keep this inside for a bit longer until it grows stronger, or plant it straight outside in the ground, or in a big garden pot in a sunny spot.

Step 7

Watch your tree grow! An apple tree grown from seed might not bear edible fruit (at least not until you are a teenager) but it will provide shelter and important habitat for animals, insects and birds.

If you liked this story
why not read the
Uncle Pete series...

DAVID C. FLANAGAN

UNCLE PETE
AND THE FOREST
OF LOST THINGS

ILLUSTRATED BY WILL HUGHES

9781916205451